# The
# Perioddicals

# The
# Perioddicals

*Geoff Meadows*

THE CHOIR PRESS

First published in the United Kingdom in 2021 by
The Choir Press

ISBN 978-1-78963-191-3

Imagine that you have a drone, a very large drone, one that you can ride, and that you take it to Ravenscourt Park on a warm sunny Sunday afternoon in April, when you have decided that doing your homework is far too dull and that tidying your room like you had promised your mum is even worse than that.

You climb aboard, twiddle the controls, lift off the ground and fly up, up over the park, across the duck pond, past the swings and the roundabout, the ice cream van, and look down on the roofs of all the houses. In most of these houses there will be a family. Some will be happy, some will be sad, some will be a little mad and others, well, just boringly normal.

And if you turn left and then carry on just a little further, you would see a surprisingly leafy road, a surprisingly quiet leafy road. And at the end of that road you would see a rather grand period building, of apartments.

Of course, by now you might be wondering if it

was a good idea after all to climb aboard a drone and to be flying with no previous experience, 50 metres up in the air.

But let's not worry about that now. After all, Hammersmith Hospital has an excellent A&E department and it is probably the best excuse you will ever have for not revising for the test on Monday. And that's even if you survive the fall.

So, you fly on, maybe a little closer to the ground now to be safe, and onwards to have a better look at this rather lovely property. Something is drawing you towards this building, and using your best and only recently acquired aviation skills, you start your descent.

But you come down way too fast and both you and the drone land in a heap, knocking over the contents of Mrs Bullen's food waste bin that she had only just that moment put out for the dustmen. And it ends up all over you, the pavement, and her cat.

There's nothing like the smell of last night's food waste on your jeans. It sort of lingers and hangs around. Like that boy at school when you have just bought a packet of Maltesers at the tuck shop and he stands there, sad eyed and looking hungry. You give him two just to make him go away.

Why did Mrs Bullen have to order a takeaway last night?

Now your new jeans are all messed up and Mrs Bullen's cat, Buster, that was once all so fluffy and white, now has the distinct odour and colour of chicken tikka all down one side.

Mrs Bullen can't have been hungry last night, or the helpings at the Monkey Temple Balti House are very generous. Either way, this is not a good look for you or Buster.

Perhaps you should have just gone out and ridden your bike, perhaps you should have stayed in and done your homework and tidied your room like you said you would. Never mind, you survived and so did your drone ... and the cat.

You pick up some of the bits that have fallen off, fold in the propellers and park the drone behind a little wooden bench where the overhanging trees will hide it from view.

So, on to have a better look at this strange and rather grand old building, with its long and wide front and two windows at the top that are set above all the others. Something is strangely familiar about it, daunting yet interesting at the same time. And you just know that you have to find out more.

And either because of feline curiosity, or because he has nothing better to do on a Sunday afternoon, but most likely because there is a piece of tasty leftover chicken stuck on the back of your leg,

Buster wants to come and find out more with you. Cats *really* like chicken, they just can't help it. Some like crisps too. And kids *really* like adventures.

And just for a moment, you both stop there in the road and give each other that long, silent, steely eyed look.

You know that look.

When you know that you really shouldn't be doing what you are about to do next, but you know that you are going to do it anyway.

Like a pair of cowboys in an old movie, standing outside the saloon in the blazing sun, about to find out who really is quickest on the draw. And sadly who isn't.

Or when Arnie says in the Terminator, 'I'll be back.'

Or when your little brother looks at you across the table when you are having a family lunch and you just know that he's about to deliver a silent and deadly fart and then blame you.

That look.

Ok then. You've come this far. Perhaps just a quick wander up to the outside of the building and a look through the windows will be enough, after all, you don't want to get in trouble and you do need to be back home in time for tea. Especially today, because on Sunday Mum likes to watch

Strictly, so it is always a pizza to save her time and that happens to be your favourite. Dinner is served at 6pm and then you are banned from anywhere near the TV so that Mum can revel in the all the sparkle and romance of the show.

Quattro Stagioni and Bruno Tonioli, you've never been sure which one is the name of the judge.

Up towards the entrance you both go, you are feeling excited and alive, but scared too. People do say that you can smell fear. If that is true, then right now it's remarkably like a mixture of mango chutney, natural yoghurt, tomato puree, a hint of chilli powder and masala paste.

There are tall metal railings surrounding the front of the property, black and pointed at the top, rusting, showing signs of age. Beyond that lies the front lawn and a short winding path leading up to a pair of heavy oak doors with a big cast-iron knocker.

Above the front doors is a stone porch and a date: 1869.

So, the building is 150 years old. Built 100 years before man set foot on the moon. Those brave astronauts who flew all that way in a tiny little spaceship to stand on the surface of another celestial body.

You reflect on this for a moment. It really does put your own flying skills to shame, but maybe it's just a matter of practice.

The gate opens with a rusty creak and Buster leads the way up the path. It does have a sign on the gate that says 'Private Property', but cats seldom appear to have any regard for such formalities and he saunters up the path as if he owns the place. By now you are feeling like you should turn back and as you approach the front doors you see a row of buzzers and some names next to them, mostly faded through time.

This really is not a good idea, you should go back and put your curiosity to one side. Buster, however, has no intention of leaving and once again he looks at you with his unblinking large green eyes.

You are in this together, remember.

The writing on the row of buzzers is small and rather hard to read and you lean in closer to the porch for a better look. It is so very quiet, except for the sound of your own heartbeat pounding in your ears.

Suddenly, the door swings open!

'Ah you are here, why didn't you knock?'

The door has been opened by an old man with a large grey beard. Well he didn't actually open it with his large grey beard, he probably used his hands, but that's not important now.

'Anyway, come in, come in.' Buster isn't shy in stepping into the house and seems to go completely unnoticed by the old man as he leads the way into a rather grand hallway.

'I assume that you are here with the catering company, though you look rather young. And by the look of your clothes, inexperienced too. You are supposed to be serving the food, not wearing it, am I right?'

The old man speaks very fast and with a strong accent, he sounds Russian, or maybe Polish, you are not sure.

You take a moment to study him, quite tall and

7

distinguished, his long grey hair swept back off his face. He wears old-fashioned clothes, smart but quite worn and with a small tie and very shiny black shoes. He doesn't wait for a reply, which is just as well as you don't know what to say.

'Well never mind, the others are not here yet. Whilst we wait, I have something that might get those ugly stains off of your clothes. Come with me, you need to look presentable today.'

You and Buster, who saunters silently at a discreet distance (cats seem to be very good at sauntering) follow the old man along a corridor and down a short flight of steps to a large door that opens into quite the most extraordinary room that you have ever seen.

The room on one side is covered by a bookcase that is stuffed full of books, some neatly placed and others piled on top of each other. Some are open and all of them look pretty ancient. As old as the building itself, perhaps older.

On the other side of the room is a window to the garden and in the corner is a large old-fashioned white sink and draining board, a bit like the one in the art room at school. Except for the fact that this one isn't exactly white. It is heavily stained and looks as though it hasn't been cleaned for years. More shelves contain every shape and size of bottles and containers, each one of them filled with liquids and powders, potions and lotions, in every shade imaginable.

But it is the middle of the room that is most interesting.

On a large bench sits a seething mass of bubbling glass tubes, expansion vessels, bell jars and flasks, rubber tubes, all connecting one to another in a seemingly endless confusion of laboratory equipment, hissing and fizzing, with a flurry of green steam coming out of one end, funnelled to a piece of old hose that leads across the ceiling and out of the window.

But above all, the one thing that you notice more than anything else in the room is the smell in there. It is horrible.

The smell doesn't just hit you when you step in; it is more like it hits you, then reverses back over you, stands you up, brushes you down and then hits you again.

It smells of, well, everything really. Bad eggs, rotten vegetables, old dustbins, wet dogs, gone-off fish, your brother, sweaty feet, dirty socks and just a hint of cheese. Mouldy cheese.

'I know what you are thinking,' said the old man, 'but you get used to it and after a few years, you don't notice it. Well not as much. Anyway, don't worry about it, it's probably not that toxic and what doesn't kill you only makes you stronger.'

You are not sure about that last statement: those cowboys in the movies that turned out to be the second fastest gun in the West didn't usually look stronger when they had lost the gunfight.

'And ok it might smell just a bit but let's just see what it can do. I only finished this formula today and I need to test it out in a live trial.'

The old man wanders over to the end of the mass of hissing tubes, disconnects one end and a green, slimy substance dribbles out into a glass beaker that he has in his hand.

He walks over towards you and then pauses, scratching the top of his head whilst looking at the liquid in a thoughtful way.

'Perhaps I should just check it on something inanimate first.' He goes over to the sink and pours the contents in.

For a few seconds nothing happens. Then, a green haze starts to circle and rise up, accompanied by a noise that sounds like really sticky tape being pulled off glass. As you stand there watching intently, the weird liquid begins transforming the sink to its former glory.

For several seconds you stand there, admiring the transformation, until tiny cracks start appearing and the sink begins to craze and crack all over.

He sighs and put down the beaker, with a disconsolate look on his face.

'Never mind. I will try again tomorrow. So if you don't mind, we will have to leave your trousers as they are.'

It is a relief. Given a choice, stained jeans are better than disintegrated ones.

The old man sighs again and resigns himself to the fact that his experiment hasn't quite worked.

'Pardon me, I didn't introduce myself. my name is Dimitri. I am the caretaker here. I live down here in the basement and I look after this lovely property. Isn't it wonderful? But in my spare time I have been working on developing a cleaning product. Not one of those that kills 99.9% of all known germs. That's easy, so obvious. Everyone does that. I am working on creating one to focus on just the other 0.1%.

'Imagine a little bottle, that is stuck to the side of every bigger bottle of detergent, guaranteed to kill the 0.1% that the big bottle cannot manage. Wouldn't that be so wonderful?'

You are not sure that most people are really that bothered abut the 0.1%, but you nod and smile and hope that Dimitri succeeds in his quest one day. That's as long as the smell in his lab doesn't kill him before then.

You both turn to leave the room when suddenly a smashing of glass makes you both jump. Buster has leapt up on to the shelving, clearly to take a look at all the various potions, lotions, bottles and jars, and his tail has dislodged one or two, sending them crashing to the floor, the contents spilling all over the place.

In the midst of the mess, one jar is spinning around slowly, having survived the fall.

Buster jumps down and runs under the table, his body low to the ground, staring at them both with those large green eyes. Dimitri wanders over and, pausing only to collect a dustpan and brush from the corner, begins to sweep up the mess.

As he does, you pick up the jar that survived and that has now stopped spinning. You look at the old dusty label and wipe it clean with one finger so that you can read it. Written in neatly flowing handwriting in faded blue ink on a yellowing label, it reads: Monkey Dust (Assorted). That's weird, where would you find monkey dust?

Dimitri seems to have read your mind and very carefully takes the jar from your hand as though it is something precious and delicate.

'I had this sent to me from the Zoological Society some years ago. They collected it for me from the cages at Regent's Park. I want to study its properties.'

Well that's even weirder. To be honest, we all like monkeys, some people even keep them as pets, your brother spends most of time behaving like one, but a study of their dust? Now you are beginning to think that Dimitri needs to get out a bit more.

The mess is now cleaned up and you both start back upstairs. Before you do, Dimitri places the jar of assorted monkey dust down next to the seething twist of pipes and tubes that are still bubbling away. The smell hangs in the air like a fog that just won't clear.

'Come along. We have so much to do, the party begins soon.'

You both go back upstairs. Buster, now looking a little less feline and a little more, well, sheepish after his accident, follows slowly behind. Back upstairs in the hallway, the light seems so much brighter and the air smells so much fresher.

Dimitri stops and looks at you. It's like he is seeing you for the first time, he slowly wipes his glasses on his very thin tie to clean them so that he can have a better look at you.

'You and your very strangely coloured cat, you are not here with the caterers at all are you?'

You are not sure what to say, you think that first of all you should tell him that it's not actually your cat, and that the strange colouring is in fact only temporary, but that is not really that important. And if you told him that you flew here on a drone, well, that's not going to sound too convincing either.

You cough to clear your throat to speak, but Dimitri interrupts before you begin. 'I know exactly what brought you and your cat here, my young friend. Curiosity brought you here today. Not the hope of earning a few pounds, standing in a striped apron, handing out very small sausages on even smaller sticks on tiny paper plates to people who are not hungry …

'No, it was curiosity, that relentless, restless urge that burns within you to learn, to understand, to make sense of everything around you. I like curious people. Curious people invent things, create things, make discoveries, push boundaries. They take risks, that is good.'

At this point, Buster recalls reading in one of Mrs Bullen's newspapers that she puts down by his litter tray, that curiosity also killed the cat. But he decides that this may be just fake news; Mrs Bullen after all does read some very poor-quality publications.

Buster does like a good read. He dictated a letter to the *Times* once on the very subject of the paper that is put down for cats:

'Sir. It is a point that I feel I must raise on behalf of the feline fraternity, that most cats of a literary persuasion both appreciate and are grateful of the fact that their custodians think to put down a newspaper or magazine, so that one has something to read during our private moments in the litter tray. However, without wishing to sound ungrateful, it is a matter of some regret and frustration, that often this just is a couple of pages torn out from a longer article and either the beginning or the end is missing.'

It didn't get published.

'And curious people are always most welcome here. So, you and your cat must stay as my guests and enjoy the party today, come, please, we are wasting time and we have so much to do, for today is a very special day!'

# The Garden

The hubbub, hustle and bustle that precedes a party began almost as soon as Dimitri put his glasses back on.

The doorbell rang with a loud and sombre 'dong' that echoed around the rather grand entrance hall and feeling that, as you were now officially invited, you should get involved and start helping out, you go to the large, heavy front doors and heave them open.

As you open the doors, two rather similar look-ing ladies dressed in black come rushing in together like a whirlwind, arms full of bags and flags and paper plates, both speaking to and above each other, bickering and a bit shouty. They are in such a tearing hurry and it's such a surprise that it completely takes your breath away and for a few seconds you feel quite light headed.

They leave behind them an assortment of napkins and streamers that they have dropped and you follow along behind them, picking them up like discarded litter. As they whoosh their way

down the hallway and out towards the garden, they shout their introduction to you. 'Hello my dear, I am Mona.'

'And I am Di.'

Taking a moment to catch your breath, you take a better look at the grand entrance hallway. It is beautifully decorated, with a long sweeping staircase and a marble fireplace, a tall and beautifully painted vase standing proudly on either end.

On the wall above the fireplace you see a very ornate silver frame and inside the frame is an old certificate that is written in a foreign language, faded by time.

Whatever it is for, it looks most important and very prestigious.

You stand on tiptoes and stretch up to try and get a better look and just as you struggle to make out the name of the recipient, the loud doorbell rings again and it makes you jump.

Dong!

You heave the heavy doors back open again, to find two short and rather burly looking men. One has a large red clipboard in his hand and the other one has a very large and shiny bald head.

He's not actually holding the bald head.

'Hello matey,' says the one with the clipboard. 'Sorry we are late. We are the party poopers. Where would you like us?'

Now, you are not the most outgoing person and you have not been to that many parties in your life, but certainly enough of them to know that no one really wants a party pooper in attendance at their event, never mind two of them.

You are about to say that perhaps they have the wrong address when you see their lorry parked at the end of the path with a portable toilet on the back.

'Look, just sign here and we'll do the rest.'

They trudge off back to their lorry to start unloading and you close the heavy doors as they go.

You look back up the hallway and see a very distinguished looking gentleman descending the staircase.

He is gliding down the stairs in a swift and graceful manner, a very tall man, wearing a blue blazer and striped tie, with glossy black hair, almost as shiny as his very shiny black shoes.

His blazer has a monogram on the breast pocket, a golden H woven into a discreet pattern, with a red silk handkerchief poking out from the top.

'Good afternoon to you,' he says in a very posh voice. He holds out his hand and gives you a firm handshake.

'I am Henry, but everyone here calls me H. I live up on the top floor of the property in flat number 1. They do insist on calling them apartments nowadays, how terribly American, but to me it's always been my flat.

'Well I must say, what an absolutely perfect day for our little celebration, and so lovely of you to join us. Gosh, it's all rather exciting. Now, I am not sure if anyone is looking after you, so let me take you under my wing and show you to the garden, you look a little hungry if you don't mind me saying. Let's get you a cold drink and something to eat.'

You follow H down the hallway, into the large bright kitchen, which is a hive of activity.

It seems that there are people everywhere, slicing and dicing, chattering and laughing, whilst they prepare food and drinks for the party, all of them so busy that you and H have to weave your way through, H greeting people as he makes his way in and out of the commotion, pausing for the odd air kiss and shake of hands as you progress towards a pair of large French doors to the terrace and out into the garden.

You step out onto the terrace with a plate of sausage rolls, cheese, a small sausage with an even smaller stick in it, some crisps and a glass of lemonade that H has picked up for you on the way through the chaos of the kitchen.

The sun is shining and you stand there in its warmth, taking in the view of the large garden and everything that is being set up for the party.

Tables are already in place and chairs are being positioned next to them.

A stage has been built for musicians. A keyboard, guitars and a drum kit are already on stage and there is someone at the mike with a handful of cables. 'Testing, testing, one, two, one, two.'

A stilt-walker in extremely long and flowing striped trousers with a red top hat and glittery waistcoat is getting himself ready, and over in the corner a juggler is rehearsing with two oranges, three apples and what looks like a rusty chainsaw. Risky.

Some people wearing brightly coloured tee shirts with 'Party Paraphernalia' on the back are hurriedly hanging up the last few strings of coloured flags.

A large BBQ is set up on one side of the garden and a faint wisp of smoke is already rising from it. The smell of charcoal and the anticipation of the tasty food that awaits wafts gently around the garden.

Things look almost ready; the party must be due to start soon.

In the midst of the activity stands a very small lady with a very large voice which she is using to coordinate the team of helpers.

'Helen!' she shouts over to a rather sweaty looking red-faced girl. 'Are you nearly done with blowing up the balloons?'

Helen looks just about exhausted and you are not surprised. She is blowing hard into a very large and shiny 'Happy Anniversary' balloon, inflating it faster than you have ever seen anyone blow one up before. She adds it to a huddle of others that already have strings attached and are floating and wafting about in the warm afternoon breeze.

You follow H as he walks over to meet the small but loud head of Party Paraphernalia.

'Ah, now you must be Miss Bottom, how delightful to meet you at last and I must say, what a splendid job you have done for us.'

'I am so pleased that you like it. You must be H, lovely to meet you too, and please, call me Ophelia.'

H nudges you forward with his arm. 'And this is my young friend, oh, please forgive me, I didn't ask you your name?'

You would respond, but you have a mouthful of tasty sausage roll, so try and smile as best you can and attempt a sort of awkward one fingered handshake whilst trying to balance a plate in one hand and a drink in the other, spilling most of your lemonade onto the leg of your jeans that managed to miss the altercation with Mrs Bullen's chicken tikka.

'Well H, I think we are just about finished setting up, shall we get the music on and get things started?'

Miss Bottom gathers her team together and they clear their steps and other equipment out of the way, just as the musicians step up onto the stage and start to play a lovely Sunday afternoon song, one of your mum's favourites, 'Fields of Gold'.

The lilting music, the sunshine and the smell of the BBQ combined has a magnetic effect and soon the garden starts to fill with the residents of the house and their guests.

Before long the lawn is crammed full of people and you look for somewhere a little less crowded to sit down.

The stilt-walker is now up on his feet, towering above everyone else, wandering around the garden, occasionally lifting his top hat and revealing some glittery juggling balls which he juggles whilst wandering around on his very, very long legs.

You see H approaching the stage, straightening his tie and stepping up onto the platform with a small piece of paper in his hand.

The band stop playing and H takes the microphone.

'Ladies and gentlemen, boys and girls. Can I have your attention please for just a moment or two? I have a few words that I would like to say on behalf of all of the residents here today. First of all, welcome to our home, so kind of you to come here to celebrate with us on this most auspicious day. And thank you to everyone who has worked so hard to make this occasion so special. Thank you and please, let's show our appreciation.'

Everyone applauds politely.

'As you all know, we are here to celebrate the anniversary of this lovely house, a house that has become our home and is of course so precious and familiar to all of us, built and completed 150 years ago this very week. We are all so proud and happy to be living together here, as many of us have done now for so long. But there is one person that we have to thank for making our community as ordered and structured and as comfortable as it is, that makes us feel like we will always belong here. And that person, of course, is Dimitri.'

A much louder round of applause rings out from the crowd and H calls for Dimitri to come forward.

There is a pause and people look around for the old man, for a moment there is no sign of him, then he appears, still wearing his apron and wiping his hands on a napkin, clearly quite uncomfortable with all the attention.

He steps up onto the stage and H hands him the mike.

'Comrades, thank you for your kind words, but they are not necessary. It has been my pleasure, you might say my duty, to do this, and seeing you all here now together on this day, where we all feel so at home, makes me feel proud of my achievements, thank you.' He gives a small bow and strokes his long beard.

Another round of applause and Dimitri quickly shuffles off the stage, keen to get out of the limelight and back to his basement laboratory.

The music starts up again and as you go back to your little patch of lawn in the sunshine, you see Buster carefully weaving his way through the forest of partygoers' legs, straight towards you.

It is now very warm and as you pull your jumper up off over your head, you wonder what the temperature is.

As if reading your mind, a very smart middle-aged woman in a grey suit and mirrored sunglasses wanders by, and seeing you taking off your jumper, introduces herself as Helga.

She then goes on to tell you that she lives in flat number 80 and answers the question you hadn't yet asked.

'Yes, is it warm isn't it? 25 degrees, warmer than forecast, but cooler later, dropping to 18 degrees at 9pm. Wasn't it cold last week though? Only 16 degrees. Just like me, must be something to do with my age, my temperature is always up and down too, up and down, just like a yoyo, never stopping still for long, oh well, never mind.'

And with that she rushes off, fanning herself with a paper plate.

Buster makes his way over to join you on your little patch of lawn and stretches himself out in the warm sun.

You watch him and reflect on the fact that cats seem to have a remarkable ability to look more relaxed than just about any other creature on Earth.

You both lie there for several minutes in silence, watching the events in the garden unfold, and you wonder about this strange and eccentric mix of characters, residents and friends who are here in this rather lovely property.

What drew them to live together here and what drew you here to be in the middle of this event today?

Buster is also absorbing it all and you watch as he slowly looks around the garden like you, observing it all with his large, green unblinking eyes.

He then turns to face you and he fixes you with that look again. 'Do you realise that you haven't yet told me your name?'

You are so utterly shocked and surprised that your mouth opens to reply, but no sound comes out.

'You didn't know that I could speak? Well of

course I can speak, what do you think that cats do when they want to communicate with someone, bark like a dog? "Oh look,"' he says in a mocking tone, '"my owner has come home, woof woof! I think there is an intruder in the garden, woof woof! Could you let me outside to do a little wee wee, woof woof!"

'Really, please, how ignorant and one dimensional the canine community are. I'm bilingual actually, I speak Welsh too. I just choose to communicate only to those with an inquisitive and open mind, who actually want to listen to what I have to say.'

Now, in a day of pretty unusual events, this seemed really peculiar. You wonder, why would a cat that lives in Hammersmith need to speak Welsh?

You regain the power of speech after the shock. 'You'll be telling me next that you can sing too?'

'Well funnily enough,' said Buster, 'I used to have a fine Baritone voice. Up until the day that the revolting Mr Bullen took me to the vet to have me neutered, and that made my voice go up two octaves and well, that was that. My place in the nocturnal choral society was taken from me. Do you know, I wasn't even consulted beforehand about the procedure, no consent forms to sign and don't even speak to me about the post-operative care. I was treated like, well, an animal.'

He shakes his head and flicks his tail around as if to try and erase the painful memory.

'I really do despise that horrible man. It has changed me in many ways. I used to be quite nocturnal. But since the procedure, I now find that I prefer to just stay in at night and read.'

The thoughts and recollection of Buster's unfortunate and life-changing procedure have clearly upset him and he is now looking unsettled.

'I think I should go and find Dimitri and see what he is up to, he should be here with everyone, enjoying the celebrations.'

# The Laboratory

B uster sits for just a few more minutes with you, doing his best to lick the remains of the chicken tikka from his fur.

Once he is happy that he has returned his look to that of an all-white cat, he then gets up, slowly stretches and gives you another one of those long looks.

'I will see you later on. Enjoy the party,' he says as he leaves your side, leaving a distinct whiff of curry breath that hangs in the air after he has gone.

You watch him as he swiftly and silently weaves his way through the dancing legs and feet and disappears back into the house.

Buster wanders through the now largely empty kitchen and, feeling a little thirsty, jumps up onto the worktop to lap up some champagne from a half empty glass, which incidentally turns out to be prosecco, not at all suited to his refined tastes.

He screws up his nose and makes his way downstairs to look for Dimitri.

At the bottom of the stairs he looks left and right and down the corridor, sees an almost closed door with the initials DM in faded ink. Yes, this is the right room.

The smell as he gets closer confirms this. He nudges the door open and goes in.

Dimitri is sat on a stool at his bench, surrounded by books and handwritten notes, paper everywhere.

Behind him on the larger bench sits the array of tubes, vessels and pipes, still hissing and bubbling away, kept alive from the chemical reactions and the small burner at one end of the bench.

Dimitri looks disconsolate, his chin resting on his hands and his long grey beard covering some of his notes.

Buster jumps up on the bench and finds a clear spot close to him. He sits upright and looks at the old man, his clothes and his ancient books spread around him and the packed shelves covering almost every wall in the room.

He wonders just how old he is and for how many years has he lived here, and what is troubling this man.

Dimitri looks up from his notes and the two of

them gaze at each other for a moment or two in silence.

'Belosnezhnyy kot. What can I do for you?'

Buster slowly licks his paw and wipes his face and his whiskers. Dimitri watches Buster do this and strokes his beard at the same time.

All is quiet except for the bubbling background noise from Dimitri's failed experiment. Buster gives Dimitri that intense, unblinking green-eyed look.

'I would like to help you,' he says.

If Dimitri is surprised by the fact that this snow-white cat can speak, he really doesn't show it.

Instead, he sits up straight and takes off his glasses, wiping them on his tie. He waves his arm and gestures to the contents of the room.

'I have lived a long life and I have studied, researched and seen many things. My life's work has taught me always to look for the unexplained, to search for the unexpected. Well, today is the first time that the unexpected has come looking for me. A cat that can speak. Einstein has his silent black hole, now I have a talking white cat. This is indeed remarkable.' He starts to laugh at his own humour. 'A very remarkable day indeed.'

Dimitri places his glasses back on his nose and stands up, straightening his waistcoat.

'When I was a small child back in Siberia, my

father once said to me, "Always let your imagination run away with you, it is what it is for." Since that day, I have remembered those words and I have spent my life dreaming, imagining, searching, questioning, trying to make order of things and to know and understand how everything works. It is such a joy when you succeed, but the pain when you cannot, it drives you crazy, you want to know the answers and yet you can't find them. Perhaps I am just getting too tired, or too old.'

He sighs and sits back down. 'Look at these books, these notes, years of study and work here and yet I am, my furry new friend, no further forward. I want to find the formula for the 0.1% and I fear that it will never be revealed to me.'

Buster looks at the notes spread out on the table. He has never been much one for detail, he is more of a 'bigger picture' type of cat and in any event, it's all in Russian anyway. But sensing Dimitri's pain, he spends some time politely looking at the documents on the desk, stifling a yawn with his long fluffy tail.

After several minutes he looks at Dimitri and jumps down off the desk and wanders around the room looking at the countless jars and bottles stacked on the shelves.

'You have tried everything in here, every one of these chemicals, substances, liquids, gases?'

'Yes, I think I must have done, it's all here in my notes, but with my work looking after the residents and this grand house, there is never enough time.'

Buster jumps up on the large bench and slinks along the side of the experiment, trying not to dislodge any of the apparatus.

He sees a jar at the end of the bench, the one that survived the accident earlier. 'What about this one?' he says.

Dimitri walks over and picks up the jar.

'Monkey dust. Well, no, I don't think I have, I have not had time to carry out any research on the properties, its chemical constituents. I can't use this, it would be pointless.'

But Buster is not giving up.

'What have you got to lose, isn't it worth a try at least? And if it is a waste of time, we can go back upstairs and join the party. Remember that you are supposed to be celebrating today, not spending the day here in the basement with me. Go on, try it, a little pinch, just to humour me and then you can close your books, switch off the Bunsen burner, we can go out to the garden and enjoy the sunshine and the celebrations. Dimitri, I can see that the people here are already proud of you, and of everything that you have already achieved in your life. Your friends are all here. So, come on, let's do it ... Dimitri. Live now.'

# Back at the Party

You have enjoyed the sunshine and watching the activities unfolding before you.

Everyone looks like they know each other and are busily engaged in conversation or just having a dance and a drink. You have often heard your mum say that she was at a party and that there was a great atmosphere. Now you know what she means, the atmosphere here is so good that you can actually taste, smell and feel it.

Everyone … except for one very pale pretty girl in a Superman shirt, sitting quietly under a tree in the shade, all by herself.

You cannot help but wonder why, so you summon up the courage to go and speak to her.

She watches you approach and looks apprehensive. Perhaps this is a big mistake and you should just awkwardly ask her the time and then leave her alone.

But as you get closer, she maintains eye contact and you decide to sit down and say hello anyway.

'Hi,' you say.

'Hello,' she replies, looking at her shoes. Well, this is really not going too well so far. 'I'm Alex, nice to meet you.'

The girl in the Superman shirt really is very shy and doesn't seem that interested in engaging with you, but it's nice and shady under the tree and it would look a bit awkward now to get up and walk off again.

Finally, 'I'm Kris. With a K.'

'Do you live here, Kris?'

'Yes. I have always lived here. Flat 36.'

You are starting to struggle with what to say next when to your relief, two rather large people come slowly wandering over to share the shade with you.

'Hi guys, mind if we chill here with you?'

You are pleased to have the extra company; Kris is really hard work.

'I am Ossy and this is my compadre, Pablo.' They plonk themselves down next to you.

You hope that they are a bit more conversational than Kris.

'We are the main entertainment later, way better than this stuff that the band are playing now.'

'Hi, I am Alex. What do you play then?' you ask. 'What kind of music?'

'You will just love us, dude, we are what you might call the resident band. We both live here, Ossy he's in flat 76 and me, I'm down the corridor at 82. Our band, we are the Electron Shells, and we are into heavy metal man, and I mean *really* heavy metal.'

'Yeah man', says Pablo, 'we are what you call metal heads. Metal, it's our thing.' They both nod and grin at each other.

You are not sure whether a garden party is the right place for a heavy metal set, but it's been one of those strange afternoons so far, who knows.

Kris with a K looks really uncomfortable now she has more people sat close to her, she moves further away and looks like she just wants to be left alone.

You are starting to wish that Buster hadn't now left you, and feeling a bit like it might be time to think about leaving, when H appears and comes over towards you.

'Ahh, there you are my young friend, I hope you are having a good time, looks like you are making friends. Hope you have had something to eat, don't be shy, go and help yourself.'

You are feeling rather hungry as it happens, so you walk over to the food area where lots of people are standing around, waiting for a burger.

As you do, you hear a distant sound and feel a slight rumble under your feet. The sort of sound you hear on a nature documentary when a leopard is walking through the forest and the animals in the trees send out a distress call.

Not the sort of sound that you usually hear on a Sunday in Hammersmith: lawnmowers, DIY, kids playing, traffic, TV and often someone shouting as loudly as they can to someone else, telling them to keep the noise down.

That's weird.

Meanwhile, oblivious to all of this, Ophelia Bottom is behaving like Queen Boudica of the catering team, rushing around, barking orders to her people to keep the food and drink flowing. H gives her a big smile and a wave, and she blushes and touches her hair, smiles and waves back in a very theatrical way.

Just one table of food looks untouched and as there is no queue, so you start walking towards it when a very tanned, almost orangey coloured man firmly puts his hand on your arm, leans towards you ear and says in a quiet and serious voice, 'If I were you, I would wait for the burgers.'

'Why?' you ask. 'What's wrong with the food on that table?'

The very tanned man introduces himself as Cullem and tells you his story. He has lived here alone in his little flat at number 29 for years and says that he knows most of the neighbours pretty well.

'See that lady who is standing there by herself at the table, all dressed in black? Her name is Ashley, I am betting that she prepared all that food herself. And if I were you, I wouldn't touch one single crumb of it.'

You study her for a moment, she does look rather

grey, very serious and now you think about it, a little bit sinister.

'She lives here upstairs at number 33, been here for years. She was married once, to a lovely fella, but he disappeared one day without a trace. Was never seen again. The rumour is that she poisoned him. Now, she was never charged, but I tell you, I am a cop, been a copper all my life, I have a copper's nose, and I tell you now, I know when someone is guilty, believe me.'

Whether Cullem and his copper's nose is right or wrong, you have suddenly lost your appetite and think that it might be time to go home and have your pizza, at least you know that Mum's cooking is safe to eat.

Well, usually.

You look around for Buster, but he is nowhere to be seen.

# The Breakthrough

Dimitri is standing in the lab still with the jar of Monkey Dust (Assorted) in his hand. He has spent his whole life as a scientist doing things the scientific way. Chemistry, after all, is an exact science. Why throw this approach away today and just throw in a pinch of dust into your carefully constructed formula?

Dust that you know nothing much about. Why?

Well, because today, a white cat came to your laboratory and spoke to you and asked you to give it a try.

It seems a good enough reason to give it a go. Dimitri looks at Buster and gives a little chuckle.

'Ok my little snow-white friend, I think this is a waste of our time, but I am ready to try.'

Dimitri puts on some safety glasses; Buster jumps off the bench and takes cover behind a pile of books on the desk.

'A pinch you say?' He gives the jar a little shake, unscrews the lid and sniffs the contents, the dust smells like, well, monkey dust should …

Monkeyish.

He takes a pinch of the dust and walks over to the apparatus on the table that it is still bubbling away.

There is a vessel with an open top and he slowly drops the pinch of dust inside. Nothing happens. The apparatus continues to bubble as before. Another failure. It is the way of things, don't get your hopes up, too often they are dashed. Dimitri gives a little sigh, shrugs and reaches to take off his safety glasses. He is dis-appointed but not surprised.

He turns and walks away from the bench and looks at Buster, as he emerges from behind the books across the room. But Buster can see what Dimitri has not yet seen. A reaction is indeed taking place and gathering pace. The liquids are bubbling away furiously and the colour, it is changing, from blue, to red, to green. And then the strangest sound begins to emerge from one of the expansion vessels. The high-pitched sound of what sounds like monkeys screeching in the treetops.

It gets louder and louder, so loud that Dimitri, who by now has seen and heard what is going on, has to cover his ears. The sound is piercing, scary and yet bizarrely funny too.

The reaction, or whatever it is that is taking place, is accelerating and the liquid is now bubbling furiously and steam is pouring and hissing out of every vessel.

'I must switch off the heat!'

Dimitri rushes to the burner, he knows that he must try and shut this down, before it explodes.

He turns off the gas and gets down low on the ground, it's clear that whatever is happening is now unstoppable and both he and Buster huddle together and hide behind the desk, waiting for the inevitable.

## BANG!!!

The explosion shakes the room and knocks some of the books off the shelf and most of the assembled apparatus shatters and smashes all over the floor. The ceiling lights swing wildly and the door to the lab slams shut.

Smoke and steam fill the room. For a few moments, they lie still and wait for the air to clear. When it finally does, the first thing that Dimitri notices is the smell. It's gone. Nothing, except the distant aroma of the BBQ from the garden.

When they are sure that all is safe, they both emerge and walk towards the vessels left on the bench that are still intact, Dimitri crunching across the mass of broken glass strewn across the floor, with Buster now in his arms.

Like most cats, he is a bit of a baby when it comes to loud noises.

Most of the apparatus that was on the bench is now shattered into tiny fragments spread on and around the bench, bits of twisted tubes, their contents dripping on the floor, flasks and expansion vessels lie in pieces. But in the midst of all of the mayhem, they see a small shatterproof plastic beaker and it is full of green liquid. A lovely shade of green. Very similar in colour, in fact, to Buster's green eyes, which right now are the size of saucers.

Dimitri, carefully reaches to pick up the beaker.

'Don't touch it!' shouts Buster in a rather pathetic, scaredy cat voice. He secretly wishes, like most domestic cats, that he had a more lion-like voice, but post-operation what can one do?

Dimitri, however, is not listening. His burning desire to succeed in his quest is undimmed and he just needs to know, has this worked?

He clears some debris off the bench, takes a test tube and draws off a few drops and places it in a petri dish to examine it under his microscope.

For a few moments he studies it, adjusting and re-adjusting the focus. He sits up and rubs his eyes. It looks like any other harmless liquid, uninteresting, no odour and well, just liquid like.

Buster gathers himself and is now calm, they both sit in silence on Dimitri's desk for a few minutes.

'What happens now?' says Buster.

'Well,' Dimitri replies, 'what I would normally do is test my experimental formulas on some heavily infected bacteria mould samples that I had specially prepared for this purpose in the lab, to see the effect on the germs. But they are nowhere to be seen, the explosion has left everything in such a mess.'

Buster thinks on his feet for a moment. Cats are very good at thinking on their feet. And landing on their feet too. But that's not important now.

He wipes his ears with his paw to remove a few tiny bits of debris from the explosion.

'So', he says, 'you need something to test it on, presumably something that is guaranteed to contain 100% of all known germs?'

'Yes I do,' said Dimitri, 'but we have nothing here that I can use, so we are unable to complete the experiment.'

'No problem at all. Leave this to me,' says Buster, 'I can definitely help you here.'

'But what can you do?'

'Well, I am, as you know, a cat.'

'Yes, I can see that,' sighs Dimitri.

'And all cats, dogs too as a matter of fact, have the ability to find the most disgusting germ-ridden, bacteria-infested, slime-covered, stinking items of detritus all over their territory. Now, cats, well, whilst we know the whereabouts of such unpleasantness, we tend to give it a wide berth and stay well away, after all, why on Earth wouldn't we? Dogs on the other hand, well that's a different story. They actively search this stuff out and when they find such matter, they take a very different approach. They sniff, it, and then lick it. And then roll around in it, as though the foul smell will somehow gift them with supernatural powers. And then to make matters worse, they eat it, sick it up and then lick up their own vomit! And after all of this, go back to their owners and greet them by licking their face!'

Buster shakes his head and shudders with the thought of what he has just said. 'Anyway, I digress, I can go now and get just what you need. I know this area like the back of my paw. If I go now, I will be back in a few of your human minutes.'

'Ok,' says Dimitri, 'then go, go now and I will clear up some of this mess and write down what has happened here today in my notes.'

Buster jumps up onto the bench and in two or three leaps and bounds of what even he feels is a fine display of feline athletic artistry, is out of the half-open window and gone, leaving Dimitri alone with his thoughts and his trusty dustpan and brush. The second time today that he has found himself clearing up broken glass from the floor of his laboratory.

He just hopes that the loss of so much of his precious lab equipment is not going to be in vain.

'Best not to get downhearted,' he says to himself and busies himself sweeping up the broken glass and picking up his dusty books that have fallen down in the explosion.

Buster is now back in his territory, hunting down the thing that they needed. It's pretty cool to be a cat, he thinks to himself, as he prowled around the back gardens, so familiar to him.

Whilst he knows that he has promised to be back in a few human minutes, he can't resist a quick detour, popping back home, just for fun, to bring a moment of life and death heart-stopping terror to an off-duty pigeon that he spies dozing in the sunshine by the back gate.

He is a cat after all. It's what they do.

And then, and just because he hates Mr Bullen, he goes over to the vegetable patch in the garden and has a little wee on his prize tomatoes. Buster can't help himself. Revenge is sweet, as they say. And, it would seem, smells faintly of prosecco.

It doesn't take him long to find what he needs. A clump of foul-smelling horribleness, just behind the bins at No 11.

He looks around for something to pick it up in and is in luck. An empty Snickers wrapper has chosen that very moment to make its desperate break for freedom from the back of a passing rubbish truck.

Sadly, it hasn't reckoned on the razor-sharp claws and lightning reactions of a cat on a mission. Buster leaps up and deftly plucks the Snickers wrapper from the air.

He then wraps it around the horrible germ-ridden lump, takes a deep breath, screws up his nose, picks up the package and heads off back to the grand old house and Dimitri's lab.

It isn't too far and he is soon at the lab window.

The wonderful aromas wafting from the BBQ are so enticing and for a moment he is tempted to suspend the mission and go and look for something to eat.

'Come on now,' he tells himself. Thoughts of food have to wait, he has more important matters to attend to.

Dimitri looks up from his desk where he has been writing up the experiment and sees Buster come in through the half-open window.

He carries the package over to the bench where the microscope is sitting and carefully lays it down.

He gags and does that funny thing that cats do when they want to cough up a fur ball. Once he has recovered, he apologises. 'Sorry about that,' he says, sits down and begins washing his face with his paws.

'I really don't see what dogs find so appealing about that stuff,' he sighs as Dimitri pours some water into a dish for Buster to wash out his mouth.

Dimitri pats his head. 'Well done, well done, my friend. As you can see, I have cleared up most of the mess that we have created today, and made some notes. Who would have thought that a pinch of monkey dust is such a volatile substance!'

'Yes,' agrees Buster. 'Next time, if there is a next time, I suggest you go for less of it, maybe just half a pinch.'

They both smile and make their way over to put

a piece of the foul-looking grey substance that Buster has brought back under the microscope to look at it. Under magnification, Dimitri can see that it is seething with bacteria and tiny little creatures.

Worst of all, it stinks, it really, really stinks.

Dimitri draws off a few drops of the precious green liquid with a pipette from the beaker and drops it into the sample.

He looks under the microscope. The effect is almost instant.

Not only does it appear to have killed everything, the sample has changed from grey to white and the smell seems to just disappear completely.

He looks up and smiles at Buster. 'My snow-white friend. It works! I don't know how, or even why, it works, but it works!'

He then rushes over to the sink and finds a heavily stained dish.

He drips a few drops from the pipette and waits.

Once again, the effect is almost instant. The dish where the drops land go from a horrible stained yellow, back to a gleaming white porcelain colour.

And this time, unlike the sink, no cracks, no after effects, it just works.

'Success at last,' roars Dimitri and he rushes towards Buster, picking him up and starting to dance a little jig around the lab, singing a song in Russian.

'We have done it, my little snow-white friend; we have done it!'

Dimitri is clearly overjoyed, he can finally let go all the frustration that he has been feeling that he has kept inside for so long.

He dances and jigs and twirls around and around for another minute or two and sings his funny little Russian song, until finally, out of breath and tired, he puts Buster down and slumps down in his chair for a rest.

They are back where they started, at Dimitri's desk, facing each other.

Once again, Buster licks his paw and wipes his whiskers whilst Dimitri composes himself and slowly strokes his beard.

They sit like this, looking at each other for a few moments, reflecting on what has just happened.

And then Dimitri breaks the silence.

'You made me do something that I have never done before. You made me think differently. You made me abandon some of my scientific principles and my usual analytical approach and well … just take a chance. You came in here, a cat that can speak, and let my imagination run away with me. Just as my father always said that I should. You made things change and happen faster than they ever would if I had carried on as I was. You are therefore by definition, and also by species, my inspiration for what we are going to call this wonderful new product that we have created here today. We shall call it ...'

## Catalyst!

'It's purrrfect,' says Buster.

'Your picture will be on the front of every little bottle sold, all over the world, imagine that.'

The thought of that does appeal to Buster. He has always secretly wished to be famous and have his face on a product. He is so envious of those annoying Labrador puppies who got the job of advertising soft toilet tissue. In some of his more reflective moments in the litter tray, looking at the adverts in the glossy and trashy magazines, he often dreams of being far away and famous, the face of the Fluffy Pillow Company. Or the beautiful white cat seen sleeping peacefully on the supersoftduvet.com website.

Never mind, he thinks, his face on a bottle of Catalyst antiseptic detergent instead of some stupid little dog getting the job will do just fine.

'Thank you,' he says, 'it would be an honour.'

'And now,' says Dimitri, recovered from his exercise, excited and full of energy. 'We must get back to the garden, we have so much to celebrate on this wonderful, wonderful day!'

# The Fire

The party is now really going well and the large and beautiful garden is packed with people.

Party Paraphernalia have put up strings of lights and lanterns and the garden is really buzzing to the sound of music, laughter and people just having a good time on this lovely afternoon.

The juggler and the stilt-walker have swapped some of their kit and the stilt-walker is now really showing off, strutting around on his very, very long legs, trying his hand at juggling three glittery balls and a live chainsaw. You just hope that he still has a hand left at all once he has finished.

Problem is that by now you are feeling a little bit out of it all, quite tired and really you just need to get back home. You have been out for a while now and thoughts of your homework and all your revision waiting for you back home is starting to stress you out. You decide to give it five more minutes and another bowl of crisps, some orange juice and ok then, just one more of Miss Bottom's burgers, and then you are definitely leaving.

And just now, as you cram the last mouthful of burger in to your mouth, you see Buster and Dimitri.

Dimitri looks so happy, smiling, shaking hands and hugging people, laughing. Buster is making his way towards you with his tail held high and those striking green eyes focused just on you.

'Ah, my young friend!' says Dimitri as he approaches. 'So good to see that you are still here and that you are enjoying yourself. Please, allow me,' he says, as he wipes a big drop of tomato ketchup off your cheek. 'We have some wonderful news!'

Dimitri is indeed a changed man, like a heavy load has been lifted off his shoulders. He explains what just happened in the lab, he is so excited and happy.

He picks up Buster and hugs him. 'My wonderful new friends, you have made this anniversary day even more special, thank you.'

You reflect on the fact that you haven't really done anything to help, other than well, just turn up, but hey, everyone is happy, so you go with the mood of celebration. The old man is happy and that makes you happy for him.

Buster had never been a huggy type of cat, he has always modelled himself more along the lines of the *cat that walks by himself* type of character. But he too can see that Dimitri is happy and he is definitely warming to the idea of being the face of 'Catalyst' and having his face on all those bottles of detergent. So he purrs whilst Dimitri hugs and they share the love for a moment or two in the sunshine.

What is of even more interest right now, thinks Buster, are the wonderful aromas coming from the BBQ. Perhaps now all the hard work in the lab is over, it is finally time to eat something.

He wriggles a bit and Dimitri relaxes his hug enough for him to jump down, eyeing the BBQ area with his 'feed me now look' that usually works on Mrs Bullen. Dimitri is indeed taken in by the 'feed me now' look too.

'Come, my snowy white friend, let's go and see what delicious things we can find for you to eat. You deserve it!'

You all wander over to the food area.

You notice that Ashley has not had much luck in giving any of her food away, her table is still pretty much untouched. She gives you all a false, over-friendly smile and gestures with both hands to all the treats on display, most with the film covering still on them.

'Come, do come and help yourself, or if you

prefer, I can make you a plate of some of my special treats.'

You feel a bit awkward and keep a safe distance ... 'Err, I'm ok thanks, I have already eaten.'

Her smile fades in an instant and is replaced by a scowl. You hurry past and try not to look at her.

The queue for the BBQ has now gone. You wonder for a second whether a queue for a BBQ in fact makes it a BBQQ, but that's not important now.

The stilt-walker is still enjoying himself with the chainsaw and the juggling act is starting to look pretty impressive. Dangerous, but impressive.

Ophelia Bottom is working away and making sure that her team is too.

'Hello,' says Dimitri, to Miss Bottom, 'I would like something tasty for my cat please, and also for me.'

'Well,' she says, 'We do have some of my very tasty sausages left, they have been very popular and you are welcome to try these.'

Buster is certainly very keen on the idea and rubs himself along the side of Dimitri's leg as if to tell him to get on with it, he is hungry.

Ophelia stands poised with her tongs at the ready. 'Pork, beef or veggy?'

Dimitri picks up a paper plate and napkin and leans in closer for a better look at her sizzling sausages. A little too close. Far too close in fact. The end of Dimitri's long grey beard touches the grill of the BBQ and within a second it is alight.

Although Dimitri has not yet noticed, his beard is definitely now on fire.

Ophelia sees this and in her louder than normal voice, screams and shouts 'Fire! Fire! He's on Fire!'

Dimitri has now seen and felt the flame licking at his old beard and starts frantically flapping at it with the napkin and paper plate to put out the flames. Fortunately, his beard is now extinguished but now the paper plate and the napkin are alight.

Dimitri, waves these around but this only makes it worse, so he throws them to the ground, not noticing that this is exactly where someone had left the BBQ lighting fluid.

Whooshhh!

The container of fluid had been left un-opened and bursts into flame in a cloud of fire.

'Fire!!! Fire!!!' screams Ophelia, jumping from one foot to the other, not knowing what to do.

H has been standing nearby with a drink in one hand, looking suave, calm and sophisticated, chatting to friends. His manner changes in an instant and he goes into complete and utter panic mode, screaming and running around in circles and then getting as far away as he can from the fire.

'It's a fire!!! Help, help, it's a fire, we are all going to die, someone do something!'

It is pandemonium, no one is doing anything helpful. H is in such a state of panic that he isn't looking where he was going and runs at full speed, straight into the stilt-walker. The stilt-walker already has his hands full with the live chainsaw and the glittery balls and now he has been knocked reeling backwards by H.

Desperately, and in a vain attempt to try and regain his balance, whilst avoiding the lethal teeth of the chainsaw flying past his face, he is swaying and stepping backwards ever faster, straight towards the party pooper portable toilet.

He crashes hard into this and sends that toppling over in a sort of slow-motion tilt onto its side. It goes over with a CRASH! And a horrible sloshing sound as the contents tip out inside the little cabin.

A scream and a muffled, horrified groan can be heard from inside. Some poor unfortunate person has chosen the wrong moment to have some private time in the pooper. And now he really is in the pooper. You shudder and don't want to think about what that poor individual has just been subjected to.

The band have by now stopped playing, the garden falls quiet and everyone's attention turns from the overturned toilet back to the fire, which by now is well alight.

No one speaks and the eerie silence continues for a few seconds as the flames light up everyone's faces.

Suddenly the gathering of partygoers parts as a voice from the middle of the huddle is heard, 'Let me through, come on, out of my way,' and out from the crowd, Di steps forwards, the only one who looks calm and composed.

She strides up to the fire, pauses, looks at everyone and puts down her drink on the food table, as though she has all the time in the world. And then in the midst of all the drama and panic around her, she smiles to herself in a calm, confident way ... and breathes in.

And in one long continuous breath she blows out the fire. The flames are gone. Just some smoke and the burned items remain.

'Oh you lot,' she smiles as you stare in disbelief. 'You really are such a load of big babies. Come on, nothing to worry about here. Just a little fire and look, it's all gone now.'

You really cannot quite believe what you have just seen.

It has been a weird day so far, but this is even weirder. And what seems even stranger is that no one else at the party seems that surprised. You look around and most people are going back to their conversations, the food and their drinks and well, just having fun again, like nothing happened. The band start up again and all thoughts of the fire seem to be forgotten. It's over as fast as it started and the fact that someone just blew it out – no one seems to care.

Except for the poor man crawling out of the party pooper. He is never going to forget this day. He has manged to free himself from the cabin of misery and is covered from head to toe in a coating of foul, dripping, slimy, stinky unpleasantness. He staggers to his feet and Ophelia, trying to be polite and helpful, but not wanting to get too close, hands him some napkins to wipe some of the mess from his hair and face.

Ok, you think to yourself, now it is really time that you were leaving.

Dimitri, is still looking very pleased with himself, despite his close encounter with the BBQ, and Buster looks even happier now that he has finally got his hands on a tasty sausage or two to eat.

You look around for H and see that he has calmed down and his suave demeanour has been restored.

'Thank you for the food and drink, H. I am leaving now, I really need to get home,' you say and he shakes your hand.

'So nice to meet you, I really do hope that you will come back and visit us again soon.'

Under the trees you can see Kris with a K, still sitting there, all by herself.

She is pretty. You noticed that earlier and seeing her again now, you wish that when you spoke, that you had been able to spend more time together. You look over in her direction hopefully and give her a smile and a little goodbye wave. But she does that thing that girls often do to you. She gives you that sort of half smile and a brief raise of the eyebrows, before finding that her shoes are suddenly infinitely more interesting to look at than you are.

I guess that means that Kris is not hoping that you will come back and visit soon, or, in fact, ever. Oh well. Perhaps one day you might find a girl who wants to speak to you for more than fifteen seconds.

Dimitri and Buster see you standing there and you all know that it is now time to say goodbye. Dimitri comes over and smiles, you sense that this is the happiest he has been for a very long time, but he is sad to see you go.

'My dear young friend, you are leaving us, so soon?'

You explain that you have to get back home and the three of you slowly make your way through the crowd of partygoers, back through the kitchen and into the hallway.

Finally, you are back in the hallway, where you met just two or three hours ago, but it feels like so much longer, after all that has happened.

Buster jumps up onto the chair by the fireplace and begins to wash his face and whiskers with his paw whilst he watches you both with his large green eyes.

You are standing by the fireplace in the grand entrance hall and once again you look up and notice the ornate silver framed certificate hanging there.

Dimitri sees that you are intrigued by it and want to know what it means.

He sighs, and smiles. 'That certificate, like me, is very old and also, like me, is from another time,

another place. Recognition for what I did so many years ago and what brought us all to this wonderful home. When I was a much younger man and when my quest for discovery raged and energy burned in me like a fire, not the tired old man you see before you today. But you and Buster, you have reignited some of that flame and for that I must thank you both. I will always be most grateful to you both for visiting here today. I wish that you could both stay here longer, but I understand that you must leave now. You both have homes to go to. Thank you, your visit has given me so very much.'

You thank Dimitri for inviting you in and he gives you a hug. Buster senses that it is his turn to speak.

'If it is ok with you, Dimitri, I would like to stay. I don't ever want to leave here. I don't want to go back to Mr and Mrs Bullen's house. If it is ok with you, I would like to live here with you, for the rest of this life … and the eight more that I have yet to come. You see, I have finally found a place where I feel I really belong. Not with Mrs Bullen and her terrible reading material, her awful choice of TV programmes and the bony cold fish food that she used to make me eat.' He shudders at the thought of it all. 'Or with Mr Bullen and his stupid vegetable allotment. I will never forgive him for what he did to me. I won't ever go back there; I just cannot bear the thought of it. Up until I came here to this house, I have felt like an observer of life, not a participant. But being here today I have found somewhere where I feel that I belong, in the lab, with you, and with all of these people who live here. This feels like home.'

Dimitri looks overjoyed and picks up Buster.

'Of course, of course you can stay, and together we will work in the lab and we will refine the process, take our new product and make it the huge success that it deserves!'

Buster purrs loudly and rubs his ears with his paws. 'Thank you, Dimitri.'

Buster gives you one more of his long slow looks and you all stand in silence for just a moment.

'And thank you, Alex, for our adventure today, I am so pleased that you chose to make your very poor landing where you did and for leading us here to this house.'

You feel rather sad, even though it has been a few hours together, you feel as though you have known Buster for much longer and you know already that you are going to miss him.

Buster looks at you and can read your thoughts. 'I know, I know it is sad that we are parting, Alex. I also know that you are probably thinking that you will come back soon and that we will text each other all the time. But I am a cat, I don't have a mobile. And even if I did, the lack of opposable thumbs makes texting slow and to be honest, we can be cold, aloof and distant creatures at times. So, let us just remember this wonderful afternoon and say goodbye.'

You heave open the heavy wooden doors and step out, pausing at the end of the path and looking back for one last time at this strangely familiar grand house and Dimitri with Buster in his arms and you wave.

And then the door closes with a bang ... and they are gone. Out of your life again as quickly as they appeared.

You slowly walk back over to the bench and the trees where you hid your drone.

You feel so tired, it is getting late and you need to get moving, but decide to sit down on the bench for just a few minutes and close your eyes whilst you reflect on what you have just experienced, this bizarre and wonderful house and the people living here.

What a strange afternoon and such a weird mix of characters.

The debonair H, Mona & Di, the fire, the resident band, Ossy and Pablo, the scary Ashley and her dubious party food.

Kris, who has a K, but absolutely no interest in you.

And of course, the old man, Dimitri, and his lab, chasing a dream to find the formula to kill the.01% that other detergents can't.

And Buster the talking cat. Now that really is the weirdest thing of all.

And why does this house seem so familiar to you, when you have never been here before?

But everyone seems happy and having a good time.

Buster has found a new home, which is great. Will Dimitri's new formula change the world of cleaning products, will anyone care? Who knows?

Whether the old man had indeed discovered a fabulous new product that was going to change the world or not, you just don't know.

Maybe all these brands that say that they kill 99.9% of all known germs just say that to avoid a legal argument and a knock on the door from those wonderful lawyers like the ones who work at Fleecem & Scarper.

You remember what your dad told you once about lawyers and the one he was using when he and your mum got divorced. He told you that they had promised on their website when he hired them, that they would: 'Separate the assets from the arguments and allow you both to move on.'

They certainly did that. They charged so much in fees, that they ended up with all the assets. Mum and Dad just ended up with the arguments.

Anyway, whatever the outcome, Dimitri is happy and Buster has found a new home where he can be happy too. And as for you, well you have had a pretty extraordinary afternoon and one that you will always remember, even if Buster forgets all about you.

You are exhausted, happy and a little over-whelmed by it all.

So you decide to stay a few more minutes to have a little snooze on the bench in the warm afternoon sunshine before you head back home to Mum.

As you drift off into sleep, you hear the music coming from the house change, the heavy metal set has begun and a huge cheer goes up from the garden as they start playing a cover of Metallica's best song, 'Cyanide'.

It makes you smile.

As your lovely nan used to say, 'It's been a funny old day.'

# Back Home

You are gently awoken by the feeling of a few drops of warm summer rain and an even warmer breeze on your face, and you realise that you must have been asleep for a while. You wipe the raindrops from your cheek and yawn. Slowly you open your eyes and try and focus.

What you see looking straight back at you sends a shiver down your spine.

Because it is not warm summer rain and the gentle wafting of a warm summer breeze that has woken you up. It is hot dog breath and saliva, dripping onto your cheek from the open jaws of Vinnie, who is staring down at you, his shiny black menacing eyes and massive teeth just inches from your face.

Your heart is in your mouth as you recover from the shock and try and remain calm. You are not asleep on the bench. You are lying on your bed, at home, surrounded by your books … but mostly by Vinnie.

You tell yourself that he is not going to eat you.

Not today. If he was, he would have already started. He is probably going to eat you another day, but today he is just here to terrify you, as he usually does.

You try and think, what is the best thing to do to get him away from you? But your head is all fuzzy from a mixture of having just woken up and the immediate threat of imminent death.

And then your mum calls out to you from the kitchen, 'Alex! dinner's ready! Come on love, Auntie Elsie and Uncle Ron are here to see us.'

Vinnie doesn't have much in the way of communication skills, but he recognises the word 'dinner' and is off, bounding down the stairs,

leaving you alive and able to sit up and recover from the shock.

Vinnie is a German shepherd dog that belongs to your Auntie Elsie and Uncle Ron. He is massive, with thick black fur, a huge head, enormous teeth and paws like a heavyweight boxer's fists.

You are not entirely convinced that he is actually a dog at all. Either there was a terrible mix up when a zoo was shipping a small grizzly bear, or he is the result of some hideous dog/bear mutation that went wrong and resulted in a Vinnie. You just hope for the sake of mankind that there is only one.

You get up off your bed, quickly put your books back on your bookcase and head downstairs for dinner.

'Hello dear! How are you? Oooh, my goodness, you get taller every time I see you, doesn't he, Ron? Come here, give your Auntie Elsie a hug.'

Auntie Elsie is lovely. She is big and blonde and, as usual, is wearing a flowery patterned dress and smells of lavender and sweets. She loves giving everyone a cuddle and always has a great big smile on her face whenever you see her.

She loves everyone and has kindness beaming out of her like heat from a fire.

She volunteers at the church and is a St John's

Ambulance volunteer, knows all about first aid and helping people.

Mum told you that she was at a Chelsea match once and on the way home she saw a man fall onto the tube train tracks at the station. Even though there were loads of people there that could help, no one did. So, Auntie Elsie quickly climbed down on the track and helped the person get back on the platform before the train came. Without a thought for her own safety, she saved his life.

She has been friends with your mum for years, not a real auntie, but you love her. Ron is her boyfriend and he is nothing like her at all. He looks swarthy and tough, with slicked back hair. He smells of cigarettes, engine oil and a whiff of menace. He is most definitely not the kind of person to help lift someone off a train track. He's much more the kind of person that would put them down there. Really not someone to be messed with.

You don't actually know too much about Ron. He never says very much, but you think that someone once told you that he is in the 'information-gathering' business. Persuading people to share knowledge. You imagine that the knowledge that he is gathering is important and very personal, things like: the whereabouts of their safe, their cash and valuables. Where they would like to take their last breath. That sort of thing.

Ron and Elsie, an odd combination. One good person, one evil one and one enormous and terrifying dog/bear. Ron loves Elsie and Elsie loves Ron. And Vinnie; well he loves them both. Everyone else he seems to view as his next victim.

You all sit around the table and Mum serves up the pizzas as she chats away happily as Mum always does and tells everyone to tuck in. You can't really enjoy your pizza though, as Vinnie is hovering right next to your chair. His eyes are boring into you, watching your every move.

Perhaps if you feed him most of your dinner, he just might let you live. You are not supposed to feed him, but you don't want to risk upsetting him, so you keep sneaking slices of pizza to him, out of fear, not kindness.

You often think about Vinnie. You thought about him just the other day at school when you were in English and you were all reading William Shakespeare. When he wrote those words in Julius Caesar, *'Cry havoc and let slip the dogs of war'*, you were sure that Vinnie was precisely the kind of beast that he had in mind. You then wonder if Shakespeare had himself been terrorised by a dog as a child. Who knows? Perhaps that's why he stayed in his room and wrote so much, not wishing to risk a chance meeting with his nemesis on the mean streets of Stratford-upon-Avon.

You thought of Vinnie every day last Christmas, hoping that Ron and Elsie weren't coming to make a surprise visit, or if they were, that they would leave him at home, to eat their furniture and whatever else took his fancy.

You are not sure that dogs even understand the meaning of Christmas, kindness and goodwill to all men. Well he certainly wouldn't understand that part. But if dogs do know that it is a time for receiving gifts, then all he would really, really want, would be a late-night home intruder. Santa outfit or not, he would be shown little mercy.

Finally, the meal is over, though you are still hungry as you haven't had much of yours, so you leave the table whilst Vinnie is distracted and have a bar of chocolate and a biscuit to make up for the pizza you didn't really have.

Mum and Elsie are having a chat about religion and people they used to work with whilst they clear the table and start tidying the kitchen.

Ron says that he is taking Vinnie for a stroll. Presumably so that he can walk off your dinner, so you escape back up to your room at last, shut the door and feel secure in your sanctuary.

Safely back in your room, you sit on the bed and think about the bizarre dream that you had earlier. You remember it all so clearly that you can almost touch it. The grand house that feels like somewhere you know. Dimitri and Buster. The smell in the lab. The BBQ fire, the party pooper incident, it all seemed so real. And yet so strange. You think about it all and you wish that it was Friday afternoon again.

But it's Sunday eve. School again tomorrow and you haven't done your homework or the revision for the test. And now it's too late, you have to go to bed. You wonder why you do always do this to yourself. Why can't you be disciplined just for once and stick to the homework diary and prepare properly?

Because it's so dull and you just don't really like school, and school doesn't really like you. So many subjects, too much homework and hours of hours of lessons studying boring stuff like simultaneous equations or the wheat plains of Canada.

You keep being asked to 'find X' in maths, but you don't want to find it, you don't care about it. You just want it to stay lost and leave you alone.

You don't like most of the kids either, they are nerds or weird, or just boring.

Why don't they teach you more useful and

practical things like how to speak to a girl … instead of learning the merits of a motte and bailey castle. It is 2019 and they don't make them anymore, so why do we need to know how they were built? Isn't it just a big circular ditch with the earth piled up in the middle and a big wooden hut perched on top?

You don't know what you want to do when you leave school but you would really love, given the chance, to become a racing driver. Fast cars, lots of money and travelling all over the world, now that must be a wonderful life. You lie on your bed and picture it all in your head, Monaco, the sunshine, Ferraris and a world of speed and glamour.

Here you go … dreaming again … not doing your homework.

You get up and brush your teeth, draw your curtains and get into bed.

Soon you are asleep … and dreaming of a far more exciting life than the one you are living right now.

# The Test

The alarm wakes you at 7am Monday morning, and it's time to get up. You yawn and stretch, shout back to Mum to say 'Yes' you are awake and crawl out of bed, into the shower.

You have exactly 43 mins from stepping out of the bed to leaving the house. Your morning has been carefully timed to maximise the sleeping time and minimise the allotted time for your journey to school. Shower, dress, look for your tie, find your kit for gym, pack your school books, eat some toast, have another look for your tie, look under the sofa for your shoes, have another more frantic search for your tie and finally, with 18 seconds to spare, pick up your packed lunch, grab your phone, tie your shoelaces, give Mum a hug and say thanks as she hands you the tie that you can never find without her help.

You only have five mins leeway, a late train or bus and panic sets in. Unless you can make up the time by running flat out for the last half mile like Usain Bolt when he *really* needs the loo, you run the risk of being late. If that happens, then you join the other sad pathetic victims of the wicked Mr Komatsu.

Mr Komatsu, or plain old Komatsu as everyone calls him when he's not around, is a maths teacher. That would make him bad enough, but on top of that, he is the teacher that handles all lateness and runs the detention class. Whatever the school is called where teachers go to learn how to be evil to their future students, he must have been top of the class there.

His job, or probably just his hobby really, is to appoint prefects to stand at the school gate and on the dot of 8.45am take the names of every pupil who hasn't crossed the line of the tarmac at that point once the bell has gone. Sometimes, he stands there himself, with his sinister smile and his watch in his hand, willing the hands to move faster as he watches the late-comers, sprinting in vain down the last 100 metres before the bell sounds, his face in a rictus grin as they fail to make it across the line.

Then, once your name is on the list, it's assembly and then off to a meeting with him to give your excuses and try and wriggle out of one of his 'mixed experience' detention and circuit-training sessions. Never normally works. Once you are late, you are late and you've had it.

His part of the experience is enjoying watching you all suffer after school in circuit training. Your experience is to simply to survive it without passing out. Once the agony of the circuit class is over, there is part two of the agony. A post-exercise warm down session, consisting of a 500-word essay on something like 'Why you should not be late for school' or 'The benefits of getting up early'.

Anyway, today does not look like one of those days, the train is on time. You make your way to school and on the way hope, just hope, that your chemistry teacher, Mr Davies, won't be there today and the test will be cancelled. Perhaps if you keep your fingers crossed, avoid stepping on cracks on the pavement, don't walk under any ladders and see two magpies on the way, then he will be off sick.

Or could it be that a velociraptor has been magically reincarnated in the night and snatched him away from his bed to feed to her young.

No such luck. You turn the last corner and as you approach the school gates, you can see his funny little car parked in its usual place, the little red dragon sticker on the rear window, there to remind him of his wife, as he once told you all.

Your heart sinks, oh well, you think, it's your own fault, fail to prepare and prepare to fail as they keep on telling you. It's into the classroom for registration and then onto assembly. The usual stuff being read out by the headmaster, you are not listening anyway, not sure that anyone ever is.

And then off to chemistry for the dreaded test.

You all file into to the classroom and take up your usual places, All the nerds line up neatly at the front, the no-hopers lounging at the back, chatting and looking like they just don't care.

You take up your place in what might be called the 'strugglers' section', about three quarters of the way back, where you think the teacher can't see you and pick on you to answer a question.

Mr Davies comes in, short and dumpy, walking quickly as he always does, thick black glasses, starched white lab coat, his white hair sticking out at the sides like a mad professor. He is not your favourite teacher; only the nerds up the front like him.

'I do hope you have all spent plenty of time over the weekend revising,' he says and starts handing out the test papers.

'Oh yes, Sir,' says Burton, sat front and centre, the grovelling, nerdiest teacher's pet of the front row. 'I hope you have made it really difficult this year, Sir, I am looking forward to this.'

What a creep. You wonder if that velociraptor could visit his house too one evening and do us all a favour. You doubt that even his parents would miss him that much.

The papers are placed face down on the desk and you all sit there waiting the clock to reach 9.15am.

You look out of the window. It is a beautiful day outside and as you watch the birds flying by, you think about your dream and the drone and wish you were out there with them, or back with Buster, instead of stuck in here. You feel anxious and have that knot in your stomach that you always get before a test.

The clock ticks' round to 9.15 and Mr Davies tells you to read all the questions carefully and to begin.

You turn over the paper and write your name at the top. And check the spelling. At least that part has gone ok.

You look down at the questions and the words just swim before your eyes, this is not good. You look away from the paper and out of the tall classroom windows. How you wish you could escape from all of this. Come on now, you say to yourself, concentrate, focus, calm down, do what he said, read the questions before you do anything.

Question 1.

What is the atomic symbol for Hydrogen and what is its atomic number? Well that's not too hard, you think, I can do that one.

H 1

Question 2.

Mercury is the liquid used in most thermometers. What is its atomic symbol and atomic number?

Oh well, you think, at least you have one right and you have spelled your name correctly. That's got to be worth something.

Come on now, think. Thermometers, temperature goes up and down ... like that woman at the party, what was her name ...? That's it: Helga. Helga in her silvery grey suit.

Helga ... who lived at flat number ... 80. She lives at number 80!

HelGa ... Helga, **HG 80.**

You write it down, this is so weird, you just feel that it is the right answer. You look back at question one, **H1.** Henry at the party, everyone calls him H and he lives at flat number 1. H, who was so terrified when the fire started.

What is going on? Question 3.

Name two heavy metal elements and give their atomic symbols.

Now you are really starting to feel a bit light headed; you are in a chemistry test and you are actually starting to answer questions. Calm down, Alex, you say to yourself. Take a deep breath.

Two heavy metals. The band from the party! Pablo and Ossy, **Pa**B**lo** and **Os**sy! They told you what flat numbers they lived in.

You know this, you know this!!! Lead **PB 82,** Osmium **Os 76.**

Question 4.

Now this one looks harder ...

The noble gases. Why are they called noble gases? Name one and give its chemical symbol.

Think, Alex, think ... somewhere lurking in the back of your mind, you know the answer to this, you remember doing this in class or reading this in your textbook.

A noble gas is one that doesn't react with anything.

The answer, it must be there, at the party, an unresponsive recluse... wait, you know this!

It's Kris with a **K.** In a Superman shirt! The answer is ... **Krypton**!!! Question 5.

Carbon Monoxide and Carbon Dioxide are both colourless, odourless gases containing carbon and oxygen atoms. But only one of them is both poisonous and flammable. Name this gas.

You can do this, two very similar gases, but slightly different ... just like the two ladies who came in through the front doors together like a whirlwind and took your breath away. Of course! **Mo**na and **Di**!

And then when the blaze started at the BBQ, Di put out the fire, just by breathing on it. So, the answer has to be Carbon **Mo**noxide!

This is amazing, you are on a roll and quickly scan the rest of the questions. You don't know the answers to all of them, let's be honest, you say to yourself, that's the sort of thing that only happens in absurdly unrealistic children's storybooks.

You run through the rest and answer a couple more. Name an extremely poisonous element. Of course, the highly dangerous and best-avoided **As**hley. Arsenic.

The symbol for a metal that has an orangey colour and conducts electricity, of course ... it's

Copper, the policeman who saved you from her, **Cu**llem.

You are buzzing with self-satisfaction and excitement. You are going to pass this test, a first in your life!

You don't understand how this happened, but it has and you are so happy. Mum is going to be happy too.

You finish the paper and there is time left. You look around the classroom.

The nerdy teacher's pets at the front are still writing away, whilst the no-hopers at the back have given up and put down their pens long ago. They are now usefully using their time screwing up little bits of paper as tightly as they can and with the aid of elastic bands firing them as hard as they can at the backs of the heads of the kids in the front row, each time Mr Davies turns his back.

A stifled giggle is heard every time they hit the target. Someone once said that the pen is mightier than the sword, but they hadn't reckoned on the power of an elastic band in the hands of the kids in the back row.

You sit there pondering what has just happened. You really can't quite make sense of it. You know the answers to the paper.

You turn the exam paper over and take out a

pencil and as best as you remember, idly start to sketch the front of the grand house that you dreamed of only yesterday, with all its windows to the flats inside. And just two little windows at each end of the building that stick up slightly above the all the others.

Soon enough the clock ticks around and Mr Davies tells everyone to put down their pens.

'Ok everyone,' he says. 'Now collect your things and bring your paper up to me and remember, no talking until you have left the classroom.'

For the first time ever, you feel very proud of yourself as you gather your things and make your way up to Mr Davies' desk at the front of the classroom.

You are usually in a rush to get out of there. But not today. Today you feel very different.

As you wait your turn to hand in your paper, you look behind Mr Davies desk at what is pinned up on the wall behind him.

The periodic table.

All the elements neatly laid out in rows, with their atomic numbers and symbols.

You look at the shape of the table and the little sketch that you have drawn of the house that you dreamed of yesterday.

You realise that the table and the sketch look the

same, the same outline, lots of little windows. Hydrogen up at the top left, where Henry lives at flat number 1.

And at the bottom of the table on the wall is a description of the person who devised it. Back in 1869.

There is a picture of him, an old man with a beard. A Russian chemist and inventor. And his name, his name is Dimitri. Dimitri Mendeelev.

'Alex. Alex, your paper please.' You realise that you have been standing there for a few minutes, mouth open, in a daze.

Everyone else has left and Mr Davies is now standing in front of you with one hand out, waiting for you to give him your exam paper.

You apologise and hand it to him, as you do so, he takes off his glasses and looks at you. That long slow look that somehow seems so familiar. And then he smiles.

And for the first time, you notice that he has very green eyes. And a little tiny Welsh dragon on his tie.

Also, that he smells very faintly of chicken tikka masala.

The end.

CPSIA information can be obtained
at www.ICGtesting.com
Printed in the USA
BVHW031745150221
600168BV00001B/25